Causes of the Civil War

Wendy Conklin

Associate Editor
Torrey Maloof

Editor
Wendy Conklin, M.A.

Editorial Director
Dona Herweck Rice

Editor-in-Chief
Sharon Coan, M.S.Ed.

Editorial Manager
Gisela Lee, M.A.

Creative Director
Lee Aucoin

Illustration Manager/Designer
Timothy J. Bradley

Cover Designer
Lesley Palmer

Cover Art
John Steuart Curry/
Kansas State Capitol, Topeka
The Library of Congress

Publisher
Rachelle Cracchiolo, M.S.Ed.

Teacher Created Materials
5301 Oceanus Drive
Huntington Beach, CA 92649-1030
http://www.tcmpub.com
ISBN 978-1-4333-0545-0
© 2010 Teacher Created Materials, Inc.
Reprinted 2013

Causes of the Civil War

Story Summary

John Brown is an abolitionist who believes he has a calling to end slavery in any way possible. He begins in Kansas, where he kills several unarmed proslavery men. Then, he raises a small army of men who go with him to Harpers Ferry, Virginia, to start a revolution. Harpers Ferry is a gateway to the west that has mountains where the army can seek refuge. He takes over the United States armory in the middle of the night. Colonel Robert E. Lee and Lieutenant Jeb Stuart arrive in Harpers Ferry to put down the rebellion. In the end, John Brown is captured, tried, and convicted of treason.

Tips for Performing
Reader's Theater

Adapted from Aaron Shepard

- Don't let your script hide your face. If you can't see the audience, your script is too high.

- Look up often when you speak. Don't just look at your script.

- Talk slowly so the audience knows what you are saying.

- Talk loudly so everyone can hear you.

- Talk with feelings. If the character is sad, let your voice be sad. If the character is surprised, let your voice be surprised.

- Stand up straight. Keep your hands and feet still.

- Remember that even when you are not talking, you are still your character.

Tips for Performing
Reader's Theater *(cont.)*

- If the audience laughs, wait for them to stop before you speak again.

- If someone in the audience talks, don't pay attention.

- If someone walks into the room, don't pay attention.

- If you make a mistake, pretend it was right.

- If you drop something, try to leave it where it is until the audience is looking somewhere else.

- If a reader forgets to read his or her part, see if you can read the part instead, make something up, or just skip over it. Don't whisper to the reader!

Causes of the Civil War

Characters

John Brown
Watson Brown
James Redpath

Robert E. Lee
Jeb Stuart
John Henry Kagi

Setting

This reader's theater begins in Virginia at the execution of John Brown. The story then goes back in time to Brown's home in Kansas. After giving an interview to James Redpath, Brown makes his way across the nation to raise an army. He decides that Harpers Ferry, Virginia, is the perfect place for a slave uprising. But, things go terribly wrong when the United States Army, under the command of Robert E. Lee, confronts Brown. The story returns and ends at Brown's execution in Virginia.

Act I

James Redpath: It does not seem possible that in a few minutes John Brown will meet his death in the gallows.

Jeb Stuart: Colonel Lee, did you see the coffin on the horse-drawn wagon over there?

Robert E. Lee: That is Brown's coffin. They want to be able to take his body away as soon as this is over.

Jeb Stuart: There was some talk in town this morning that the hand of God would snatch him from his cell and take him straight to heaven.

James Redpath: I have heard whispers that there are armed men hiding in the forest around here. They are waiting to rescue Brown and take him away.

Robert E. Lee: No matter where I go, I see newspapers like yours, James, that tell the story of Brown.

Jeb Stuart: I heard that he only grew the beard after coming out this way to Harpers Ferry. He wanted to disguise himself.

Robert E. Lee: One thing I know for sure, people are passionate about what they think of Brown. Some people call him a madman. But after today, he will be a martyr.

Jeb Stuart: How can anyone look at Brown as a hero? Don't they know that he is responsible for brutally murdering unarmed men?

James Redpath: I have been writing about John Brown for a few years now. At one time, I thought of Brown as a hero. I met him for the first time just three years ago. Let me tell you that story.

Act 2

Watson Brown: Father, James Redpath is here to see you. He is a reporter from *Harpers Illustrated Magazine.*

John Brown: Yes, son, I have agreed to speak with him.

James Redpath: Mr. Brown, thank you for allowing me to come to your camp in Osawatomie.

John Brown: Mr. Redpath, this is my son, Watson. And this is John Henry Kagi, my second in command. I am glad you are here. I want my message to be heard by all so that I can build my army.

James Redpath: What message is that, Mr. Brown?

John Brown: Slavery is a national sin that stains the souls of all Americans. No American can expect to be saved from hell until slavery is abolished. I will start a race war, one that will wipe out slavery.

James Redpath: Watson, is this view shared by your entire family?

Watson Brown: Mr. Redpath, Father was raised by an abolitionist. It is all he has ever known.

John Brown: Watson is right. When I was only 12 years old, I stayed with neighbors who owned a slave my age. The boy was ill-clothed and poorly fed. He had been separated from his parents and was confused. It is hard for me to talk about this.

Watson Brown: Father, allow me. The boy made a small mistake, and his owner beat him senseless with a shovel.

John Brown: I will never forget that beating. I was too young to say anything. But from that day on, I swore that I would wage an eternal war on slavery.

Watson Brown: By the time Father was 20 years old, he had already helped one slave escape to Canada. I am very proud to say that our house was a station on the Underground Railroad.

James Redpath: There are so many other well-known abolitionists. Why haven't you joined with Northern abolitionists like William Lloyd Garrison or Frederick Douglass?

John Henry Kagi: They are all talk and no action. This talking will not break the grip that slavery has on this nation.

John Brown: I see myself as a warrior of God. He has sent me to destroy this wicked institution of slavery.

Watson Brown: Mr. Redpath, you must understand that Congress has only hurt the slaves. It passed the Fugitive Slave Law. This law allowed the South to keep its slaves. It also stated that the Southerners could cross over into Northern states when slaves tried to gain freedom by escaping.

James Redpath: I see what you mean. I wrote about the Dred Scott case. The Supreme Court ruled that slaves are not citizens and have no rights.

Watson Brown: We were pleased when the Kansas-Nebraska Act was passed. This act allowed the people living in Kansas to vote to decide if the state would be a free state or a slave state.

John Brown: The Kansas-Nebraska Act was my invitation to war. I decided to move to Kansas with my sword in hand ready to smite down those who stand for slavery.

James Redpath: I know that there is a warrant out for your arrest. Some people say that you and your sons massacred innocent people. Surely, there is a good reason for this. Can you tell me what happened?

John Brown: Mr. Redpath, you must understand that I have a higher set of laws that I must obey. I am answering God's call. If blood must be shed to end slavery, then God will smile on this blood.

Watson Brown: The massacre that you speak of, Mr. Redpath, was because of those proslavery Missourians.

James Redpath: What do you mean?

John Henry Kagi: Most people around here call them Border Ruffians. They live in Missouri, but they cross the border to vote for Kansas to be a slave state.

Watson Brown: We are members of the Free State Party, a political party that opposes slavery. Anyway, there was a shoot-out between an antislavery settler and a proslavery settler over their farm boundaries.

John Henry Kagi: This shoot-out started a war between the Free Staters and Border Ruffians.

James Redpath: I remember my magazine covering this event. They called it Bleeding Kansas because so many people died. But didn't the Free Staters get enough votes to make Kansas a free state?

John Henry Kagi: Yes, eventually Kansas became a free state. But this made the Border Ruffians angry.

Watson Brown: The Border Ruffians organized one more despicable act. One of them, a federal marshal, led 800 men into Lawrence, Kansas.

James Redpath: Why Lawrence, Kansas?

Watson Brown: Lawrence is the center of Free State activities, including antislavery newspapers. In Lawrence, they looted homes, set a hotel on fire, and destroyed the printing presses of two antislavery newspapers.

John Brown: I have no patience for timid antislavery Americans. So, three days later, I led a small band of seven men into Pottawatomie, Kansas.

Watson Brown: I was with Father and the others that night. We visited the homes of several proslavery activists.

James Redpath: Mr. Brown, the reports say that you were armed with guns and razor-sharp swords. What happened that night?

John Brown: We knocked on the doors. I announced that I was captain of the Northern Army and that I intended to take these proslavery men prisoners.

James Redpath: Were these men armed?

Watson Brown: No, they did not have any weapons, but these men were evil. They were for slavery, the cruelest form of human treatment. They all deserved to die.

James Redpath: Did their slaves break free and follow you?

Watson Brown: No, these men did not have slaves, but that does not matter. The fact that they were for slavery is what matters.

James Redpath: Are you worried about being arrested? Do you know if the law is on your trail?

Watson Brown: We are not afraid of being caught. After all, Kansas has no organized police force.

John Brown: I only have one short life to live and only one death to die. I will die fighting for this cause. There will be no peace in this land until slavery is abolished.

James Redpath: Thank you, Mr. Brown. I am leaving here with more respect for the Great Struggle than I have ever had before. I feel that I have just met the leader of the second and holier American Revolution.

Poem: Brown of Osawatomie

Act 3

John Brown: From studying those maps and military books, I am sure this is the divine place. These mountains around Harpers Ferry will be our stronghold where we can strike at our enemies.

John Henry Kagi: Harpers Ferry is perfect. It has a large arsenal right down the road where rifles are made and stored. This extra stash will come in handy. Our army can carry all the firearms to the mountains where we can establish our fortress.

John Brown: That is why you are my second in command, Kagi. You think just like I do. Do we have enough funding to help us buy more guns and ammunition?

John Henry Kagi: We have a good amount. I have purchased 200 rifles, 200 pistols, and 1,000 pikes. Most slaves will not know how to use guns, so we had these pikes made especially for them. All this was purchased with money from the Secret Six.

Watson Brown: Do you mind me asking, who are the Secret Six?

15

John Henry Kagi: The six are Gerrit Smith, the man who gave us the farm in New York; Thomas Wentworth Higginson, the minister and editor of *Atlantic Monthly*; Dr. Samuel Gridley Howe; Minister Theodore Parker; Franklin Sanborn, the teacher; and businessman George Luther Sterns.

John Brown: Each one has told me that under no circumstances should I reveal their ties to me.

John Henry Kagi: They are urging us to go back to Kansas and continue fighting there. But, it appears they are willing to look the other way while you do what you must to end slavery.

Watson Brown: They preach freedom, but they always stop short of a fight, don't they, Father?

John Henry Kagi: These men are weaklings and do not have the stomach to do what must be done.

John Brown: I have my calling telling me what to do. And, I have their money to carry it out.

Watson Brown: They are of the same mind as Frederick Douglass.

John Brown: When I told Douglass about this raid, he pleaded with me to drop my plans. I cannot deny that I was disappointed in him, but it made me more determined to see this plan through.

John Henry Kagi: I do not have your same religious views, but I am committed to ending slavery, too. I am sure that our plan will succeed. We have 19 men with us so far. More men are bound to join.

John Brown: It is dark now. Men, arm yourselves. It is time to proceed to the ferry.

Watson Brown: I have sent two of our men to cut the telegraph lines that lead into the town. They are already coming back. It looks like they were successful.

John Henry Kagi: Watson, do you see the watchman guarding the bridge? Grab him and take him prisoner. Go!

Watson Brown: I have him! We can cross the bridge now.

John Henry Kagi: I can see candles in people's windows, and I hear the piano playing in the local tavern. No one is paying any attention to us. It looks like we can walk right up to the arsenal building in the center of town.

John Brown: I can see it right over there. There is another watchman out front.

John Henry Kagi: Go, men! Grab the watchman. That's right. Good work, soldiers. Bring him here! Stand him up straight.

John Brown: You are now my prisoner. I came here from Kansas, and this is a slave state. I want to free all the Negroes in this state. I have possession of the United States armory. We can now take over the storehouse of weapons about a half mile up the road. When we get that, we will have captured about a million dollars in ammunition and rifles.

John Henry Kagi: Sir, we should carry these weapons to the mountains and establish a fortress right away.

John Brown: No, I think we should wait here a while. A flight from Harpers Ferry could trigger a gun battle. I do not want any of these hostages killed.

Act 4

Jeb Stuart: Here we are, finally in Harpers Ferry. I cannot help but feel a little tired after riding all night. Sir, I would expect you to feel conflicted about this duty. After all, you are not for slavery.

Robert E. Lee: It is true that I personally feel that slavery is a great evil. When I was younger, I freed my family's slaves.

Jeb Stuart: Sir, have you heard who is in charge of this insurrection?

Robert E. Lee: No, I have not been given that information. It does not matter to me. I am here to carry out the orders given to me from President Buchanan.

Jeb Stuart: Sir, it is the notorious John Brown from Osawatomie. He has a small group of men, as well as hostages. He has barricaded himself in the engine house.

Robert E. Lee: Lieutenant Stuart, have you found out any details about this raid?

Jeb Stuart: Sir, I have been told that the first shot fired was heard around midnight just two nights ago, the very evening that John Brown came into Harpers Ferry. A watchman approached the bridge to work his midnight shift, only to be attacked. He fought his way free, and one of the raiders shot at him. But, he was able to get away and sound the alarm to warn the citizens.

Robert E. Lee: The newspaper is printing that all the citizens at Harpers Ferry were taken prisoner. I can see this angry mob of citizens and know that this was only a rumor. It also reported that the first one to die was a free black man named Hayward Shepherd. Is this correct?

Jeb Stuart: Yes, Shepherd is a citizen of Harpers Ferry. When Shepherd saw the armed gunmen at the bridge, he ran away. Brown's men fired at him and killed him.

Robert E. Lee: That is ironic, isn't it? Brown is an abolitionist, but his men killed a free black man.

Jeb Stuart: Sir, the white townspeople of Harpers Ferry are angry. They are passing around whiskey and yelling, "Kill them!" They can think of nothing more dreadful than a black man with a gun.

Robert E. Lee: Have there been any attempts at a truce?

Jeb Stuart: Colonel, there have been a few attempts on Brown's behalf. When Brown sent out his son-in-law with a hostage and a white flag of truce, the townspeople ignored the white flag.

Robert E. Lee: Do you mean that they killed him?

Jeb Stuart: Yes, sir, they did. They want to lynch any of the raiders that are caught. They have even shot his son, Watson. He was able to get back inside their stronghold. He must be near death.

Robert E. Lee: I have heard that anyone wanting a rifle is getting one from the arsenal. It is dangerous to leave justice in the hands of the people. The law must handle this. President Buchanan has given us a job to do, and we will do it.

Jeb Stuart: What must I do, Colonel?

Robert E. Lee: Lieutenant Stuart, I want you to carry a white flag up to the door of the engine house. I know that this is dangerous, but it must be done.

Jeb Stuart: I can do this. I will go alone.

Robert E. Lee: If Brown does not surrender, and I do not expect that he will, you must command the Marines to charge the engine house and force them out. Here, take this white flag.

Jeb Stuart: *(shouting)* I am coming in peace. I want to speak to your leader. Send him to the door.

John Brown: I am here. Speak, Lieutenant.

Jeb Stuart: I know you. You are John Brown of Osawatomie. I met you in Kansas.

John Brown: Yes, I remember when your army unit tried to stop the settler war there. What is that paper in your hand? That must be your orders.

Jeb Stuart: Colonel Lee, United States Army, commanding the troops sent by the president of the United States to suppress the insurrection at this place, demands the surrender of the persons in the armory building. If they will peacefully surrender themselves, they will be kept in safety to await the orders of President Buchanan.

John Brown: I want to be escorted out of town. Then, I can release my prisoners.

Jeb Stuart: You must surrender with no preconditions. Are you ready to surrender and trust the mercy of the government?

John Brown: No, I prefer to die here.

Jeb Stuart: Then, you have given me no other choice.

James Redpath: Colonel Lee, I am a reporter for *Harper's Illustrated Magazine*. Can you tell me what is happening?

Robert E. Lee: Just as I suspected, Lieutenant Stuart is waving his hat. The Marines are advancing just as planned. Look over there!

John Henry Kagi: Help! Men, they are battering the door with sledgehammers. Help me push the doors back and secure them.

Watson Brown: Father, I am too ill to even stand.

John Henry Kagi: Then shoot this rifle out the window. Surely you can hit some of the Marines.

Watson Brown: Father, they are now using a ladder to ram into the door. Oh, no, here they come! Stand clear!

Jeb Stuart: The door has caved in! Attack, soldiers!

John Brown: Oh, I have been stabbed!

Watson Brown: Father! He's collapsed!

Jeb Stuart: Take him and the other prisoners who are still alive to the local jail for now. I will report back to Colonel Lee.

James Redpath: I must speak with Watson Brown. Colonel Lee, do I have your permission?

Robert E. Lee: Yes, you may speak with him.

James Redpath: Sir, are you the son of John Brown?

Watson Brown: Yes, you are correct.

James Redpath: Why would you attack Harpers Ferry?

Watson Brown: Duty, sir. It was my duty.

James Redpath: Here, let me give you a drink of water. There you go. Take it slow. I have one more question. Was it your duty to shoot people?

Watson Brown: I am dying. I cannot discuss the question. I did my duty as I saw it.

Robert E. Lee: And I did my duty as I saw it. Carry him away, men. He certainly will not live past this evening.

Jeb Stuart: Colonel Lee, it is finished. Brown is injured, but not seriously. He will be held in the office next to the engine house.

Robert E. Lee: Good work, Lieutenant Stuart.

James Redpath: Lieutenant Stuart, this only took three minutes. The entire raid here took about 36 hours.

Robert E. Lee: Lieutenant, can you give me a briefing about the injured?

Jeb Stuart: Sir, there are 17 men who have been killed. Ten of them are raiders, four are townsmen, two are slaves who joined the raiders, and one is a marine. Two of the dead are Brown's sons.

James Redpath: Colonel Lee, I would like to interview Brown. Is that possible?

Robert E. Lee: Certainly, if he is willing to talk.

Jeb Stuart: Mr. Redpath, I will take you to him. He is inside this office. Mr. Brown, you have a visitor.

James Redpath: Mr. Brown, you might not remember me, but I spoke with you a few years ago in Kansas at your camp.

John Brown: Yes, I do remember. I am willing to answer your questions.

James Redpath: Can you tell us who furnished the money for your expedition?

John Brown: I furnished most of it myself. I cannot implicate others. It is by my own folly that I have been taken—

James Redpath: But you killed some people here.

John Brown: Well, sir, if there was anything of that kind done, it was done without my knowledge.

James Redpath: What was your objective in coming here?

John Brown: We came to free the slaves and only that.

James Redpath: How do you justify your acts?

John Brown: I think the Southern states are guilty of a great wrong against God and humanity. It would be perfectly right for anyone to interfere and free those whom you willfully and wickedly hold in bondage.

James Redpath: Upon what principle do you justify your acts?

John Brown: Upon the Golden Rule. I pity the poor in bondage that have none to help them. That is why I am here.

Jeb Stuart: Colonel Lee, I think this interview should be over. Can no one hear the crowd?

Robert E. Lee: Yes, they are shouting and yelling. Mr. Redpath, you need to leave.

James Redpath: It looks like a scaffold is going up. Are they intending to lynch Brown?

Robert E. Lee: I am afraid you are right. We must move him and the other prisoners right away. We will need protection. Get the men ready. We will make our way to Charles Town, just eight miles away.

Act 5

Robert E. Lee: And now here we are at John Brown's execution. His trial was a little more than three days. It only took the jury 45 minutes to decide he was guilty of murder, treason, and encouraging a slave rebellion.

Jeb Stuart: It was strange that when the verdict was read, Brown just sat there emotionless, picking his teeth with a toothpick. I must ask about something that has always bothered me. If John Brown wanted to lead an uprising, then why did he do it at a place where there were so few slaves?

James Redpath: That is a good question. I have wondered why he did not send word of his planned uprising to plantations in the South.

Jeb Stuart: There are thousands of slaves there. I am sure they would have joined him.

Robert E. Lee: I am not sure any of these questions can be answered by anyone but John Brown. And he refuses to answer them.

James Redpath: Writers in the North are hailing him as a great liberator. Others say that violence, bloodshed, and treason cannot be excused.

Robert E. Lee: Only history will judge us accurately.

Song: John Brown Song

Brown of Osawatomie

by John Greenleaf Whittier

John Brown of Osawatomie spake on his dying day:
"I will not have to shrive my soul a priest in Slavery's pay;
But let some poor slave-mother whom I have striven
      to free,
With her children, from the gallows-stair put up a prayer
      for me!"

The shadows of his stormy life that moment fell apart,
And they who blamed the bloody hand forgave the
      loving heart;
That kiss from all its guilty means redeemed the
      good intent,
And round the grisly fighter's hair the martyr's
      aureole bent!

So vainly shall Virginia set her battle in array;
In vain her trampling squadrons knead the winter snow
      with clay!
She may strike the pouncing eagle, but she dares not harm
      the dove;
And every gate she bars to Hate shall open wide to Love!

John Brown Song

Author Unknown

John Brown's body lies a-moulderin' in the grave,
John Brown's body lies a-moulderin' in the grave,
John Brown's body lies a-moulderin' in the grave,
But his soul goes marching on.

Chorus:
Glory! Glory! Hallelujah!
Glory! Glory! Hallelujah!
Glory! Glory! Hallelujah!
His soul goes marching on.

He captured Harpers Ferry with his nineteen men
    so true;
He frightened old Virginia 'til she trembled through
    and through.
They hanged him for a traitor, themselves the
    traitor's crew,
His soul goes marching on.

Chorus

Glossary

abolitionist—a person who wants to abolish (or do away with) slavery

armory—a storage place for weapons

array—to set in order

arsenal—a collection of weapons

aureole—a bright light around the head or body of a person in a picture of a sainted person

barricaded—blocked off by a barrier to protect against attack

execution—legal punishment where someone is killed

gallows—a mechanism for execution by hanging

golden rule—a rule that one should treat others as one would like to be treated

hailing—praising

insurrection—revolt or rebellion

liberator—one who sets others free

martyr—one who suffers death because of what he or she believes

preconditions—requirements that must exist beforehand

shrive—to confess one's sins to a priest

stronghold—a well-fortified place

tavern—a place where alcohol is sold and consumed